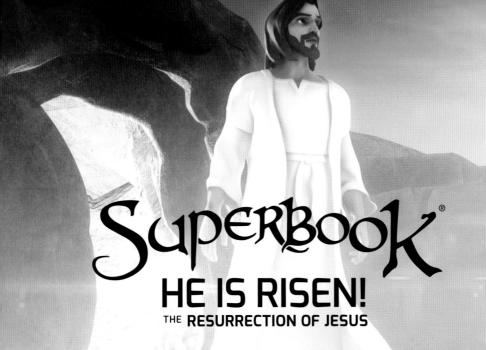

SUPERBOOK®
HE IS RISEN!
THE RESURRECTION OF JESUS

Most Charisma House Book Group products are available at special quantity discounts for bulk purchase for sales promotions, premiums, fund-raising, and educational needs. For details, call us at (407) 333-0600 or visit our website at charismahouse.com.

Story adapted by Gwen Ellis and published by Charisma House, 600 Rinehart Road, Lake Mary, Florida 32746

Library of Congress Cataloging-in-Publication Data

Names: Ellis, Gwen, adapter.

Title: He is risen! / story adapted by Gwen Ellis.

Other titles: Superbook (Television program)

Description: Lake Mary, Florida : Charisma House, [2020] | Series: CBN

  Superbook storybooks | Audience: Ages 4-6. | Summary: "Superbook

  intervenes and in a very special episode, takes Chris, Joy, Gizmo and

  Pheobe back in time for an encounter with Jesus' mother, Mary, during

  the time of her son's crucifixion"-- Provided by publisher.

Identifiers: LCCN 2019036917 | ISBN 9781629997520 (hardcover)

Classification: LCC PZ7.1.E456 He 2020 | DDC [E]--dc23

LC record available at https://lccn.loc.gov/2019036917

20 21 22 23 24 — 987654321
Printed in China

"You never told me," Chris said to his mother, Phoebe Quantum.

"Yes, I did. I told you twice. You don't listen."

"Aw, Mom, I don't want to go to dinner with Uncle Stan. He is so boring. Besides, Broken Eardrums is playing at the civic center tonight, and I planned to go."

"Well, you'll just have to miss it."

"This is so incredibly unfair," Chris said as he stormed out the front door.

Outside he went on complaining to his friend Joy and their robot, Gizmo.

At that his mother came out the front door saying, "Christopher Quantum, you and I are going to discuss your attitude right now."

Just then Superbook whisked them away—
along with Chris's mom!

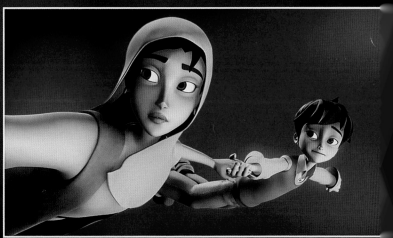

"Where are we?" she exclaimed.

"My sensors indicate the date as more than thirty years after Jesus was born. And we are in Jerusalem," Gizmo offered.

"Will someone explain what's going on?" Chris's mom asked.

"They've arrested Jesus, the Messiah," a man said, "and they've taken Him to the governor, Pilate."

"Are You the King of the Jews?" Pilate asked Jesus.

"Are you asking this on your own, or did someone tell you about Me?" Jesus answered.

"Your own people and the chief priest sent You to me. What have You done?"

"My kingdom is not of this world," Jesus said.

"Are You a king?"

Jesus said, "I came to the world to tell the truth."

"What is truth?" Pilate asked Jesus. Then he told his soldiers, "Take Him and whip Him."

The soldiers were cruel. Not only did they whip Jesus, but they hurt Him by putting a crown of thorns on His head. They made fun of Jesus and spit on Him and pulled out His beard. Then they took Him back to Pilate.

Pilate looked straight at Jesus. "Don't You know I have the power to release You or to have You killed?"

"You would have no power at all over Me, unless it were given to you from above," Jesus told him.

At that Pilate took Jesus to the crowd of people waiting outside.

"Do you want me to nail your King to a cross?" Pilate asked in a loud voice.

"We have no king but Caesar," someone in the crowd yelled.

Then all the people began to chant, "Crucify Him! Crucify Him!"

There was someone in the mob who loved Jesus. It was His mother, Mary. There in the crowd she met Chris's mom. With great fear they watched all that was happening.

Mary was heartbroken. Her Son, Jesus, had been taken by the Romans to be killed.

The Roman soldiers took Jesus to a hill called Golgotha. There they nailed Him to a cross. They would keep Him on the cross until He died.

Pilate ordered a sign to be put on the cross. It said "Jesus of Nazareth, the King of the Jews."

As Jesus hung on the cross, He said, "Father, forgive them, for they do not know what they do." He was talking to His Father in heaven. Soon darkness covered the land.

Standing with Mary and the others near the cross was John the disciple. The scene was so awful that none of them could believe what they were seeing.

Then Jesus spoke. He said to John, "Here is your mother."

John answered, "From this day forward I shall care for her as if she were my own."

Jesus was dying, and yet, even now, He was concerned for His mother.

Chris was listening and was beginning to understand what it meant to show respect for your parents. He went near his mother and slid his hand into hers.

How long could this sorrow and pain go on? Not much longer.

Jesus cried out, "It is finished." Then His head dropped forward. He was dead.

Everyone hurried away. Chris, his mom, Joy, and Gizmo went with Jesus's mother and the disciple John.

"We've been here three days," Chris said. "Why doesn't Superbook take us home?"

"Chris," his mom replied, "Mary has lost her Son. That's the worst thing any mother could face. I am not leaving her now."

"Perhaps there is something else Superbook wants us to see," offered Gizmo.

Just then the door flew open! Mary Magdalene, a friend of Jesus, burst into the room and ran up to the disciple John.

"John," she said, "I've seen Him. I've seen Jesus. He is alive!"

"How can that be? Stay here while I go check," said John, and he left.

"What happened?" Chris's mom asked Mary Magdalene.

"I couldn't sleep, so I went early to the tomb," said Mary
Magdalene. "When I got there, the tomb was open, and
there were two men—dressed in white linen—who told
me Jesus was not there. I was upset. I wanted to know
where they had taken Him. Then I heard a voice. I thought
it was the gardener, but it wasn't. It was Jesus! He called

my name. I wanted to hug Him, but He told me He had to go to His Father in heaven. He said we should go to Galilee, and He would see us there."

"Oh, wow!" exclaimed Joy.

Gizmo said, "He's alive!"

With that both mothers and the three friends were out the door to see this miracle for themselves. After all, they had seen Jesus die on the cross.

"Mary, Mary," called John as he raced toward them. "It's true. Jesus is risen! The tomb is empty. Jesus said this would happen, and now it has."

Chris's mom felt better because Mary was happy. She knew Mary was going to be all right, so she could leave now.

"Thank you for your kindness," said Mary. "May the Lord bless you and take care of you and your son." Then she turned to Chris and said, "Take care of your mother."

"I will," answered Chris. That was the very moment Superbook chose to take them home.

They landed at home at the very time that Chris had stormed out of the house. As his mom came out the front door, Chris, Joy, and Gizmo wondered if she would remember the journey to Jerusalem. But she didn't—because she said, "Chris, we are going to discuss your attitude right this minute."

Chris was thinking hard, and he remembered all the kindness Jesus had showed his mother.

"Mom, I'm sorry," he said. "I was wrong. I was totally out of line. I know how much you do for me, but a lot of times I act as if I don't. I've changed. I remember what's really important. So if you want me to visit with you, Dad, and Uncle Stan, I'm cool with it."

Chris's mother couldn't believe her ears. "What in the world has gotten into him?" she wondered. She didn't know why he had changed so much, but Joy and Gizmo did!

"For God so loved the world that He gave His only begotten Son, that whoever believes in Him should not perish, but have everlasting life."

—John 3:16, NKJV